CUENTO
DE LUZ

To my daughter Andrea, capable of illuminating the darkest forest.
- Margarita del Mazo -

To Olivia and Javier, the stars of my life.
- Silvia Alvarez -

Lucy´s Light

Text © Margarita del Mazo
Illustrations © Silvia Álvarez
This edition © 2015 Cuento de Luz SL
Calle Claveles 10 | Urb. Monteclaro | Pozuelo de Alarcón | 28223 | Madrid | Spain
www.cuentodeluz.com
Title in Spanish: La luz de Lucía
English translation by Jon Brokenbrow

ISBN: 978-84-16147-00-7

Printed by Shanghai Chenxi Printing Co., Ltd. January 2015, print number 1483-2

FSC
www.fsc.org
MIX
Paper from
responsible sources
FSC® C007923

LUCY'S LIGHT

Margarita del Mazo * Silvia Álvarez

When the sun has set, silence falls over the Big Forest, and all of the nighttime animals wake up.

In the trunk of a big, strong tree lives Lucy. She is the youngest member of a family of fireflies.

The night always lets them know it's on the way, because it doesn't like to catch them by surprise.

"Here I am!" the night says.

Then all the nighttime animals know it's their turn.

Lucy carefully watches as her family gets ready. They wave their bottoms in the air, wiggle their feelers, take a deep, deep breath, and sing, **"Here we go, it's time to glow!"**

And in a flash, they head off to light up the forest.

"I want to go too!" says Lucy.

"You're still too small," says Grandma Firefly, "but soon you'll shine just like everyone else!"

And finally, after waiting and waiting, Father Firefly says to Lucy, "Tonight you can come out with us. Are you ready?"

"You bet!" she says, excitedly.

Along comes the night, and says, "Here I am!"

The fireflies all get ready (including Lucy). They wave their bottoms in the air, wiggle their feelers, take a deep breath, and sing, **"Here we go, it's time to glow!"** And in a flash, they head off to light up the forest.

The little firefly looks around her.

A giant light, like a great big firefly, is floating in the sky, round and bright.

Suddenly, Lucy turns back towards her home, sobbing.

"What's the matter?" asks Father Firefly.

"I don't want to go out! My tummy hurts!" says Lucy.

"Don't worry, you'll shine tomorrow." says her father. "We all feel nervous sometimes." And he gives her one of those special kisses that makes everything right again.

The following evening, Mother Firefly says to her, "Lucy, it's time to shine. Are you ready?"

"You bet!" she says.

Along comes the night, and says, "Here I am!"
  They all get ready, and sing, **"Here we go, it's time to glow!"** And in a flash, they head off to light up the forest.

The moon is still there, floating high in the sky. Lucy pokes out her head, and then rushes home, sobbing.

"What's the matter?" asks her mother.

"I don't want to go! I'm tired!"

"Don't worry, you'll shine tomorrow. It's all the excitement. It gets us all muddled," says Mother Firefly. And she gives her one of those special kisses that help you go to sleep.

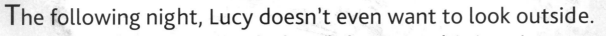

The following night, Lucy doesn't even want to look outside.

"I've got cramps in my feelers," she says. This is quite common in inquisitive fireflies, and Lucy is very inquisitive.

"It doesn't matter," says Grandma Firefly. "You can shine just the same."

"I can, but I don't want to!" says Lucy. "My light is only tiny, and it isn't any use. The great big firefly in the sky lights up the whole forest!"

"What you see up in the sky is the moon!" says Grandma Firefly.

"Then I want to shine like the moon," cries Lucy.

"Really? Then I'll tell you a secret," whispers Grandma Firefly. "The moon only shines when the sun lights it up. Otherwise, nobody can see it."

Lucy listens to her grandma, and then peers up at the moon, shining in the sky like a beautiful jewel.

"Well," says Lucy, "then we can't trust that big old moon.

But my light is important!"

And with that, she flies off into the night as fast as her wings can carry her.

In the Big Forest, when night falls, all of the fireflies shine away just in case the sun doesn't feel like lighting up the moon.